Big Bird's
RED BOOK

**Illustrated by
Michael J.
Smollin**

**By Rosanne and
Jonathan Cerf**

A SESAME STREET/GOLDEN BOOK

Published by Western Publishing Company, Inc., in conjunction with
Children's Television Workshop.

This educational book was created in conjunction with the Children's Television Workshop, producers of Sesame Street. Children do not have to watch the television show to benefit from this book. Workshop revenues from this product will be used to support CTW educational projects.